TRAPPED!

TRAPPED!

And Seven Other Stories

Joan Sodaro Waller

To order additional copies of this book, contact:
Xlibris LLC
1-888-795-4274
www.Xlibris.com
Orders@Xlibris.com
543411

Contents

I would like to dedicate these stories to my family members:

Bob
Peg, Tom, Jim,
Matthew, Christina, John, Rob,
Alexa, Taylor
Katie & Parker

Introduction

Hello! Welcome to my storybook!

The stories printed here would make wonderful picture books which I want you to create. That's why there are no illustrations on these pages.

As you read or hear the stories, ask yourself:

What do the characters look like? What are they doing? That way you will fall in love with the characters as YOU create them. Every time you think about each story, let your imagination change the pictures in your head. Later, if you like, you may actually draw those pictures on the "illustration pages" which I have provided for you following each story.

GET INTO the action. **BECOME** the characters. **SEE** the scenery and **PUT YOURSELF INTO** the story. **SMELL** the odors. **HEAR** the sounds. **FIGHT** the battles. **FEEL** the characters pain, their joy, their sorrow. **BE** there and **BE** involved. **LAUGH, CRY AND CHEER.**

It's like magic.

Try it! You'll like it!

1

Trapped

"I'm bored," Steve thought to himself. "There's never anything to do around here on Saturday. I guess I'll go over to Billy's and shoot some baskets."

He grabbed his basketball and dribbled it down the street passed the abandoned house. The stories he had heard and his Mother's warnings to stay away from it had only increased his curiosity.

When Steve arrived at Billy' house he asked him, "You know that weird house at the end of the street?"

"What about it?" Billy replied.

Steve continued, "Well, every time I go by that house, I have this strange feeling that it's calling me. Why don't we go over there and peek inside. Today I'm bored enough to even risk getting into trouble with my Mom. Let's take a look and then we can shoot some baskets."

"Heck, yes! Let's do it," Billy agreed enthusiastically.

When the boys walked up to the house, the front door opened slowly inviting them to enter, like someone was expecting them. As soon as they were inside, the door slammed shut and the bolt in the lock dropped into place with a bang. It startled them. Immediately, Steve tried to release the bolt, but it wouldn't budge.

"We'll never get this door open. Let's look around," he said as he led Billy further into the hallway.

"Boy, its dark in here," Billy commented in a shaky voice. "This place gives me the creeps. Let's get out of here!"

"Don't worry, Billy. There must be a door or window open somewhere. Can you feel that cold draft?"

"Yeah, I felt it right away after the door slammed shut," Billy remembered.

"You look for an open window and I'll look for a door," Steve suggested, leaving Billy alone in the living room.

After Billy had investigated all the windows, he said aloud to himself, "No wonder it's so dark in here. All these windows are covered with wood. They must be painted on the outside to look like curtains hanging in the windows. I'd better find Steve and see what he's discovered."

Billy stumbled around in the dark until he found Steve in the hall looking at a strange door. "This is the only other door I've found so far, but it's sealed shut," Steve informed Billy. "What about the windows?" he asked

"There's no way out through the windows. They're also boarded up tightly. It looks like our only chance is to get that front door opened."

First, they worked on the bolt. Then they beat on the door, hoping to release it. Finally, in desperation they screamed for help, but no one came and their words just echoed back at them. Realizing they were trapped in the forbidden house, Billy began to cry.

Steve was scared too, but instead of crying, he was thinking. "Let's take another look at that hall door. Maybe we can find a way to unseal it. It might lead to the basement where there's a door to the outside," he reasoned.

As they ran their hands over the sealed door and the adjacent wall, Steve discovered a strange bump. When he pushed on the bump they both heard a tiny bell ring and they felt the sealed door slide to the left. Behind the door a steep staircase appeared which was dimly lighted by a small light bulb somewhere in the distance.

Surprised and frightened, yet curious, Steve whispered, "Let's take a look."

As Steve led the way down the creaking stairs, he glanced over his shoulder and caught sight of the door quietly and slowly closing. "Billy, quick throw your body against the closing door and force it to stay open."

Billy did his best, but the only way he could make it stop was to wedge his body into the remaining space. "Steve, hurry and find something strong enough to hold the door open. I'm caught and the door is squeezing my rib cage."

Steve stumbled down the dark staircase, crawled around the basement floor and found a piece of sturdy pipe. He raced back up the stairs two at a time.

"Billy, lift up your body so I can wedge this pipe along the threshold," he said as he carefully laid the pipe between the door and the frame. "There, that ought to hold it. Now, slowly wiggle yourself loose."

Billy twisted back and forth several times trying to release his jeans which were caught on a loose screw. Finally, in desperation, he made a quick jerk which tore his jeans, but set him free.

"Are you okay, Billy?" Steve asked as he grabbed hold of his friend who almost fell down the stairs.

"Yeah, I'm fine. Just give me a minute to catch my breath and stop shaking," Billy answered as he wiped the sweat off his face with his shirt sleeve.

Then he clutched onto Steve's right arm as the two boys cautiously descended the stairs.

"Listen, Steve! Can you hear those voices?"

"Yes, I hear them. They seem to be coming from the end of that other passageway where another small light bulb is burning dimly."

When they reached the end of that dark hall, they found a boy and two little girls crouched in the corner of a dark room. The children screamed in fright at the sight of Steve and Billy standing in the doorway.

Steve raised his arms and pleaded with them to be silent. "It's okay! We aren't here to hurt you," he assured them. "But, what are you doing down here?"

All three children tried to explain at once until Steve calmed them down. Then, little by little, each one helped tell the story.

"We live in the three houses behind this abandoned house. We have always felt drawn to come into the house, but we were afraid to even come close to it," said Tommy.

Then Caroline took over. "But today, we decided to go closer and look in the windows," she explained. "Since we couldn't see in the windows, we moved towards the basement door to see if it would open."

"We were surprised when the door began to open slowly," Betsy continued. "We had barely squeezed through the opening when suddenly the door slammed shut, the bolt dropped into the latch, and we were trapped."

"How long have you been here and how did you survive without any food or water?" Billy asked.

"We really don't know how long we've been here, but we know that our parents must be really worried about us," Caroline said.

Then Tommy explained. "Once a day, we'd feel a cold draft and then food would appear, but we never saw or heard anyone. We've searched everywhere in the room, but there's no way out of here except for that basement door which can't be opened from this side. There's a latch and bolt, but no door handle."

"Well, now we know there's no way out through a basement door. So we still have to figure out how to open the front door," Steve reminded them.

Realizing that the door to the basement stairs was now open, the long-trapped children rushed past Steve and Billy and hurried to see for themselves as they clamored together up the stairs.

"Wow!" Billy exclaimed. "Those stories we've heard are true."

Steve was so quiet that Billy knew he wasn't listening.

Suddenly Steve shouted. "I've got it! I've got it!" as he pushed the children aside and flew to the front door. He slid his hand quickly over the wall next to the door. "Sure enough, here it is," he burst out joyfully as he pushed on the bump. Like magic the bolt was released and the door creaked open slowly. They were all free at last.

"Hooray! Hooray!" the children sang out, jumping up and down and stumbling over each other to be the first to escape.

When they reached the safety of the street, they stopped to glance back. A cold shiver ran down Steve's spine; he felt an unseen presence call them to return.

"Hurry!" Steve shouted running as fast as he could and leading the others away from the beckoning house. "Let's get away and let's stay away!"

Never again did Steve, Billy and the smaller children ever go close to that weird house.

ILLUSTRATION PAGE

ILLUSTRATION PAGE

2

Dinky, The Stowaway Cat

"Ho hum, another beautiful day by the lake. Where shall I nap this morning?" Dinky asked himself as Monica shooed him out for the day.

He checked out the wall near the front door, the patio, the dock beside the wide river, the boat and several of his other favorite sunny spots. Then, he noticed an old black truck parked in the driveway.

"Ah, what's this? Here's an interesting new place to sleep undisturbed. I think I'll just snuggle up on these rags for comfort," he decided and soon fell fast asleep.

"Wow, what's happening?" he meowed as he felt the truck climb up the steep driveway. Every time he tried to jump out, the truck swerved around another curve. When it turned onto the highway and sped across the river, Dinky braced himself. The wind blew so hard in his face he kept his eyes closed tightly.

"Where in the world am I going?"

"Help, someone! Help!" he cried out.

Finally, the truck turned onto a bumpy, gravel road and stopped suddenly. Dinky lost his balance and fell out. He ran back to the road.

"That was an exciting ride, but now I must find my way home. If I follow this road, it should lead me back to the bridge. I'll cross the bridge to reach my side of the river," he reasoned. "Then it should be easy to find my house in the woods."

"Good, here's the bridge. As soon as this car passes I'll follow it onto the bridge." Dinky waited in the weeds for his turn.

However, each time he started to move forward another car whipped past him onto the bridge and as trucks passed they nearly sucked him under their wheels.

"I can see my hometown across the river, but I'm afraid to cross the bridge to get there," he whined and crouched in a ditch. His legs wobbled, his tongue was dry as sandpaper, and he felt cramps in his stomach.

"I'll just rest awhile in these woods next to the wide river."

As he rested, he imagined he could hear Monica calling, "Dinky, where are you? Here, Kitty, Kitty. Here, Kitty, Kitty."

He purred, "Here I am," over and over, but of course she couldn't hear him.

"I'm hungry," he complained. "I'll check out that house over there." Dinky ate some food from a garbage can. Then he hurried off to search for a safer bridge to cross over the river.

On Tuesday, he longed to nap in the sun on the riverside. A kind old lady fed him scraps from her table, but after eating he ran off.

On Wednesday, he longed to nap in the sun along the roadside. In a barn a nice farmer fed him some warm milk from the cows he was milking, but after he'd had his fill, Dinky ran off again.

On Thursday, he longed to nap in the sun on a dock. A young boy stopped to pet him and gave Dinky half of his hot dog.

On Friday, he longed to nap in the sun in the open field. Along the roadside, Dinky found a fast-food restaurant bag full of food. After he ate it, he continued to limp along slowly.

On Saturday, Dinky turned onto a road that led away from the river and up a steep hill. Hour after hour he trudged up the hill.

At nightfall, bright lights in the distance caught his attention. "Look! There's my city!" Dinky meowed aloud. He ran as fast as he could toward it. "Home, sweet home!" his heart shouted.

When he reached the city everything looked strange. "What's wrong here? There are too many tall buildings. There's too much traffic. There's no river and no bridge."

Just then, a young lady walked by. She stopped to look in the lighted store window. Dinky rubbed against her legs and he purred softly.

She picked him up and cuddled him in her arms. "Poor Kitty, what are you doing out here all alone?" she whispered in his ear.

"You're trembling. Are you scared? Are you lost?" she asked.

Dinky relaxed and snuggled close as she carried him to her apartment.

On Sunday, the young lady took Dinky's picture for the large posters which she and Dinky tacked up around the neighborhood. It read:

FOUND: BLACK AND WHITE MALE CAT WITH CRIPPLED RIGHT BACK LEG

CALL: 555-9765

Dinky felt very important. He'd never seen a picture of himself before.

He liked living in the young woman's apartment high above the city. He gobbled up the large portions of the high-class food she fed him. He napped next to the sunny window. At bedtime, he crawled next to her and slept soundly. In fact, Dinky liked it so much he almost forgot about getting home.

On Wednesday, the phone rang.

"Hello," Dinky heard the young lady say, "Yes, I'm the one who posted the message about the lost cat. Does it match the description of your cat?" she asked.

Dinky listened.

"You say the cat's name is Dinky and he's been missing from his home in Clemson for over a week. Well, he certainly wandered far away," she said.

When the young lady mentioned his name, Dinky crawled up beside her and purred into the phone.

"Just a minute," she said to the young man. She laid the phone down and stepped into the next room.

"Dinky" she called softly. Again Dinky came over to her and rubbed against her leg.

The young lady picked up the cat and the phone. "I think you may have found your mother's cat. Would you like to come over to see if this really is Dinky?" she asked.

That afternoon when the young man arrived, Dinky went right to him.

"There's no doubt in my mind. This is Dinky," the young man said as the cat licked his face.

"Would you like to drive to Clemson with me" I'm sure Monica will want to thank you personally for your kindness.

Dinky nestled in the front seat of the red sports car between the happy, young couple. He purred quietly and fell asleep.

Images of strange trucks, winding roads and hills, crowded bridges, endless rivers, and miles and miles of lonely highways flashed through his dreams. He tossed and turned and made strange noises in his sleep.

But, when he felt two warm hands touch him, he fell into a more restful sleep. His purring grew quiet again.

This time he enjoyed dreams of himself napping in the bright sun on the wall near the front door, on the patio, on the dock beside a wide river, on the boat, and in his other favorite places near his large, brick house in the woods. Dinky purred softly.

When the car, stopped the young man carried Dinky toward the house. Suddenly, Dinky spotted a black pick-up-truck. He wiggled free and hid under the convertible.

"Dinky, where are you? Here Kitty, Kitty. Here Kitty, Kitty," a familiar voice called.

Curiously, Dinky crept from beneath the car. He looked about. When he noticed Monica standing next to the truck, he ran and rubbed against her legs purring loudly. Dinky knew he was home at last.

ILLUSTRATION PAGE

ILLUSTRATION PAGE

3

The Old Rocker And Me

"Crick, crick, crick, crick," the Old Rocker sang as I rocked harder and faster. I loved the feeling in my stomach. When I closed my eyes, I made believe I was lost alone on the open sea. The winds blew and my ship rocked on the waves, but I had to open my eyes before nausea swept over me. It's fun to make believe. I do it all the time.

That's how I got through a boring day when the other kids were in school and there was no one to play with and nothing to do. Mom was busy about the house or talking on the phone. Dad was working on his computer. The Old Rocker became my best friend. He and I went all sorts of places together.

One day we took a trip to the jungle. I brought my bow and arrows. As I rode through the jungle on the back of my friend, the Rocker, I shot at all the jungle animals who tried to attack us. I felt safe because my Rocker had a high back to hide behind and sturdy legs. When I became really frightened, I rocked as hard as I could and we moved across the jungle quite rapidly.

On days when rain kept me from playing outdoors, I pretended to be lost in the jungle in the middle of a monsoon. If I needed shelter from the terrible drenching rain, I made myself a shelter high in the top of the trees. It was easy to do. I simply turned my Rocker upside down and threw a blanket over it. When at last I was safe and dry inside my hut, I cuddled up on my side and fell fast asleep. I must have slept a long time. When I finally opened my eyes, I thought I saw a fierce looking bird staring me in the face, but it was only my big sister peeking through the opening in the blanket.

Sometimes in the winter, when the snow blocked the doors and I couldn't go outside to play, I turned the Rocker upside down and made believe that the back of it was a snowy hill. I put on my ear muffs, mittens, scarf and boots to make it seem more real. After each slide, I'd run around the house to warm up. Once I slipped on a rug and pretended I had slipped on a patch of ice.

When my brother and sister came home from school, they wanted to slide, too, but my mother put a stop to that real quick. We were getting carried away with our hilarity, laughing and running wildly around the house and sliding on the Rocker. You see, they were much bigger than me. I was only four. Molly was seven and Jack was nine.

My jungle gym was fun to play on in the spring, but when I was sick and had to stay inside, I needed to find another way to get some exercise.

Then one day I discovered that by laying my Rocker on its back I had created a miniature jungle gym. I crawled in and out of the chair's legs, braces and rockers, just like I crawled in and out of my jungle gym outside.

With the front edge of the seat now sticking upward, I imagined it was my high wire. I put a pillow case across my shoulders for a cape and a broom handle in my hands for a balancing pole and became a tightrope walker at the circus.

As I closed my eyes and pretended I was high above the earth. I could hear the crowds cheering and clapping as I put one foot in front of the other. As I came to the edge of one side, I turned around very carefully.

Then suddenly I heard real clapping. My father and mother were standing in the doorway watching me. My mother breathed a sigh of relief after I had safely jumped down off the Rocker. They gave me big hugs and helped me set the poor Old Rocker back in an upright position and put my costume pieces away where they belonged.

These are just a few of the adventures the Old Rocker and I enjoyed while I was young.

ILLUSTRATION PAGE

ILLUSTRATION PAGE

4

Who's A Fraidy Cat?

"I'm not going to climb any higher. I'm scared," Jamie admitted. Her knuckles were white from clutching the branch so tightly.

"Oh, don't be a Fraidy Cat," Kelsey chided her.

"I'm not a Fraidy Cat! You dared me to climb to the first branch. I did and I'm not going any higher."

"Look, I'm one branch above you already. Just grab hold and pull yourself up."

"No, Kelsey, I'm staying right here," Jamie said as she clenched her teeth and tightened her lips.

"Fraidy Cat! Fraidy Cat! Jamie is a Fraidy Cat," Kelsey chanted.

"It's always the same," Jamie grumbled to herself as she looked down at the ground which looked farther away than before. She closed her eyes to stop thinking about falling, but when she did her body swayed, so she opened her eyes to stop the dizziness.

"Look, Jamie, now I'm two branches above you," Kelsey bragged.

"I hate the way Kelsey pushes me into things and calls me names. If another girl lived in the neighborhood, I'd have dumped Kelsey long ago. Instead, every morning when she comes over to my house, I get sucked into her plans," Jamie admitted.

Now, as she sat glued to the branch, she remembered other times when Kelsey had challenged her to do something stupid.

"This is worse than the time she insisted that we stay in the middle of the street until an approaching vehicle climbed the hill and turned toward them. Or, how about when she talked me into paddling across the windy lake without life jackets. Well, this scares me the most because I'm afraid of heights," Jamie thought.

"Now, I'm on the fourth branch above you," Kelsey shouted.

"Big deal," Jamie shouted back wishing she could do something brave or heroic.

As she fought back the tears, she suddenly heard a branch creak and Kelsey scream.

As Jamie turned and looked up, her foot knocked the ladder away from the tree trunk. It toppled to the ground with a thud.

"Jamie, go for help," Kelsey pleaded.

"I can't," Jamie sobbed. "The ladder has fallen."

"Just let go of the branch with one hand, roll onto your stomach, push off and drop to the ground."

Jamie glanced up at Kelsey again. What had only been seconds, now seemed like hours. Jamie could hardly breathe as she imagined herself letting go of the branch and falling to the ground.

As Kelsey shifted her weight, the branch creaked some more, and smaller branches broke off and were caught in the tree.

"Hurry, Jamie, this branch won't hold me much longer."

"What if I break my leg?" Jamie thought. "What if I hit my head on the gnarled tree roots? What if . . . ?" she asked herself. She prayed for courage as she lifted her right hand off the branch and rolled over onto her stomach. The branch felt hard and ruff.

"Hurry, Jamie, hurry!" Kelsey insisted.

Jamie took a deep breath. "Please, dear God, help me," she prayed out loud as she pushed herself loose and fell backwards into the underbrush. Unfortunately, she hit the gnarled roots with her left foot.

"Are you okay?" her friend called.

But no answer came.

"Jamie, are you all right?" she called again.

Finally, Kelsey heard Jamie's voice in pain answer.

"I guess I'm okay, except my left ankle feels like it's either sprained or broken. When I put my weight on it, the pain is awful.

"Can you walk?" Kelsey asked.

"Don't worry. I'll go for help even if I have to crawl all the way. Kelsey, you just hang on tight and don't wiggle around," Jamie shouted as she crawled out of the underbrush toward home. When she tried to walk, she winced in pain every time she put pressure on her foot. But the thought of Kelsey falling from the tree drove Jamie to continue.

As she crawled over a large tree trunk that blocked the way, her foot slipped into a patch of wild grape vines. A snake slithered past her while Jamie waited motionless. Then she continued. At last, as Jamie crawled to the crest of the hill, the clearing beside her house appeared. This gave her courage. She crawled faster till she finally reached the phone inside the kitchen door.

"Mom, are you here?" Jamie shouted, but no one answered so she dialed 911 thinking, "These numbers are like a life line for anyone in trouble."

"Hello. This is 911. How may I help you," a friendly voice asked.

"It's my best friend. She's clinging to a broken branch near the top of an oak tree in the middle of the woods. Hurry! She's about to fall!" Jamie spoke loudly into the receiver.

"Is this the Wauld residence?" the woman operator asked in a calm, quiet voice.

"Yes," Jamie answered anxiously.

"Is your address 189 Mulberry Lane?"

"Yes."

"Is your phone number 211-555-9782?"

"Yes."

Jamie noticed that she felt calmer each time she responded to the lady's sweet and kindly voice.

"What is your first name?"

"My name is Jamie."

"Jamie, are you hurt?"

"Yes, I hurt my left foot when I dropped down from the tree."

"Then, just wait by your front door and the ambulance will pick you up on the way to the woods," the operator instructed her.

"Jamie you are now connected to the fire and rescue squad. They are on the way to help your friend. Please explain to them what happened and stay on the line until the ambulance arrives at your house. Good luck, Jamie, and thank you for calling 911."

Jamie explained to the men about Kelsey, but she wished they would stop asking questions and help her friend instead. "Please hurry!"

"Is Kelsey hurt?" they asked.

"No, but she's hanging onto a branch way up near the top and the branch is about to break," she said as she burst into tears.

"Don't worry, little lady, we are already on the way."

By this time Jamie's foot had swollen to twice its size and her body itched.

"Mother, are you home?" she called loudly as she crawled toward the front door to wait for the ambulance. Silence filled the house. "Mother, where are you?" she called again.

Just then, she heard her mother's car pull into the driveway. "Jamie, what in the world have you done to yourself?" her mother asked when she saw her daughter crawl out the front door dragging a very swollen foot and her body covered with scratches and red blotches.

But, before Jamie had a chance to answer her mother's questions, the ambulance attendant ran over. He picked her up and carried her to the waiting vehicle. "Mrs. Wauld, please follow us to the woods in your car," he said.

When the ambulance arrived at the woods, one fireman had already unhooked the extension ladder from the truck while others had gathered up the ropes, the stretcher, and the trauma kit. They waited for Jamie to explain where the tree was located.

"I'm sorry," she admitted. Maybe if you carry me into the woods I could find it easier.

Just then, they heard Kelsey screaming for help.

"You and your mother wait here. We can follow Kelsey's call for help. Please pray that we get there in time. We'll find her and have her back here in no time," the giant-sized fireman assured them as the rescue squad walked together towards Kelsey.

While they sat side by side, Jamie finally told her mother what had happened and snuggled close to her as they sat in the ambulance.

"I'm sorry Mom. I should never have let Kelsey talk me into this. It was a really stupid thing to do. Next time I won't be so weak."

"Jamie, I'm proud of you. Look at how brave you were, crawling all the way home to call 911 even after you hurt your foot," her mother said as she gave Jamie a tight hug and kissed the top of her head.

Jamie had almost forgotten about her painful ankle, as well as the scratches and itches, as they waited and waited for the rescuers to return.

"Here they come, Mom. It looks like they found Kelsey before the branch broke loose from the tree. Aren't they wonderful!" she exclaimed. She wanted to run to meet the returning heroes, but she couldn't stand up even with her mother's help.

"Jamie! You did a very brave thing today. I won't call you Fraidy Cat any more. I'm really sorry," Kelsey apologized and gave her friend a big hug. "Thank you, Jamie. You were wonderful," she said as tears of pain and joy rolled down Jamie's cheeks.

Turning to Jamie the woman attendant said, "Now, let's take a look at this wounded warrior." Jamie winced when the nurse pressed on her tender ankle. "It looks to me like you've broken your ankle pretty badly," the woman explained. "And, you also have a good case of Poison Ivy and we need to clean up these serious scratches before they become infected."

"You mean I crawled and hobbled all that way on a broken ankle." Jamie shook her head in disbelief. "Maybe I don't have to be such a Fraidy Cat anymore," Jamie told herself. "At last, I've done something brave and heroic."

Everybody cheered, clapped, and hugged the heroine of the day.

ILLUSTRATION PAGE

ILLUSTRATION PAGE

5

Best Friends

"Mom, when we go camping this week can Genie come with us?"
Molly asked.

"Yes, dear, you know Genie is always welcome to join us, but it
might be hard on her to be out in the weather for six days. You know
how sensitive her skin is. The sun may turn her arms and legs brown,"
her mother warned.

"I'll make sure she always has something to protect her from the
sun and the weather," Molly responded.

"That might solve the problem, Honey. That's a good idea," Mrs.
Brown agreed. "Now, help me get these camping supplies packed in
the wooden storage box."

"Mom, we sure take a lot of stuff. Do you want me to check off
each thing as I put it in the box?"

"As usual, Molly, you are very efficient. Yes, that would really
help," Molly's mother agreed.

"Let's see. We have three flashlights, one lantern, toilet paper and
tissue, two boxes of matches, dish towels, a scratchy pad, dishcloths,
cooking utensils, cups, saucers, plates, silverware, glasses, pots, pans,
newspapers, paper towels, hatchet, pocket knife, whistle, sun tan
lotion, binoculars, detergent, soap, clothespins," Molly called out as
she checked off each item. "Is that all for the wooden box?

"Yes, that takes care of the miscellaneous items. Now you can start
loading the food items into this cardboard box. You don't have to list
them," said her mother.

"After you load this box, go to the closet and collect all the outerwear, including rain coats, rubbers, umbrellas, caps, and warm jackets. You remember how cold it gets at night. I'll go upstairs and start packing the clothes."

Molly and her mother busied themselves with their assignments and soon the house looked like a tornado had struck.

Meanwhile, Mr. Brown was busy in the garage getting the tenting equipment stowed in the small trailer along with folding lawn chairs, bats and balls, hiking sticks, swimming gear, fishing poles and the Frisbee.

After Molly was ready for bed, she packed her favorite toys and quickly crawled into bed. "Mom, I really tired from all the work we did. I know I'll get a good night's sleep and Genie will, too," she said as Mrs. Brown kissed Molly and Genie goodnight.

"Wow, what a beautiful day for camping!" Molly shouted and the family agreed as they started loading the car and the trailer with the rest of their gear. At 9:00 a.m. they were ready to drive away.

"Oh! Oh! We forgot to bring the water cooler," Mr. Brown said as he jumped out of the car and ran back to retrieve the all important water cooler. "Now, off we go once more!"

Singing songs and counting brands of cars was their favorite past time. It was amazing how many songs they each knew. Sometimes they would make up new words to old melodies, like "You Are My Sunshine" and "Row, Row, Row Your Boat."

"There are so many things to do after we get there and set up camp. How are we going to choose what to do first? Dad, how much longer until we get there?" Molly asked for the umpteenth time.

"Well, we've traveled two hours so it must be about an hour till we reach Hungry Bear Campground. Just keep busy with Genie so she doesn't get bored. OK?" he suggested.

An hour later signs to Hungry Bear began to appear along the road. The weather was still beautiful.

Their camping space on the side of a small lake had many shade trees. It took about two hours to unload the gear, set up camp and eat a late lunch.

"Dad, now can we go for a hike to explore the campground, then take a swim in the lake before we light the campfire and cook dinner?" Molly asked.

"You bet your life we can," he agreed enthusiastically. "Let's put on our swimming suits and be off to explore and to swim. Grab your walking sticks and towels, too. Molly you can bring Genie. Just be sure to wrap a towel around her."

The next few days were filled with swimming, fishing, Frisbee, volley ball and horseshoe games, boating and sightseeing.

"It's Thursday. Time to go horseback riding!" Molly announced as soon as the sun rose and the campground began to come alive.

"Remember, we have to tidy up our site before we leave," her father reminded her. "Let's be sure the ice chest and all small items are inside the tent in case a storm comes up."

"Molly, I'm sorry you can't take Genie. She'll be more comfortable and safer in the tent," Mr. Brown announced after he inspected the campsite. "O.K. Let's go!"

"You go ahead. I'll catch up," Molly said as she started back to the tent. "I forgot something." She unzipped the tent flap, went inside, grabbed her jacket and waved goodbye to Genie. Hurrying, she caught up with her parents just as they were approaching the stables.

"I hope I don't get one of those nags who just poke along and nibble branches along the way. I want a perky horse," Molly said enthusiastically.

However, fifteen minutes later Molly was already bored with the slow pace of the trail ride. "When will we go back to the campground?" she asked. "I miss Genie. She must be lonesome there all by herself."

"Molly, just be patient and enjoy the scenery. We still have about 45 minutes before we get back to the stables," Mrs. Brown said.

Forty five minutes later, they dismounted their horses at last. Molly raced ahead of her parents. When she went inside the tent, she immediately raced back. "Genie is gone! Genie is gone!" she kept shouting with tears streaming down her face. "Come quickly! Hurry! Something has happened!"

Mr. and Mrs. Brown joined Molly as they all hurried to their tent where they found a disaster and no Genie.

Food from the ice chest had been tossed everywhere. Red blood from the steak had dripped on everything. The cot where Genie had been sitting was torn to shreds.

Molly just kept sobbing, choking and saying over and over, "We have to find Genie! We have to find Genie!"

"Honey, we'll look for her right away," her parents said as they both hugged and kissed their precious daughter.

"First, we'll ask the neighbors if they saw anyone enter our tent while we were riding. Then we'll search every inch of this place," Mr. Brown promised.

They discovered that all the neighbors had also been gone so no one saw or knew what had happened.

"It looks to me like this is the work of a raccoon. But I don't know how he could get in. I zipped the flap myself right down to the bottom, but when we returned the flap was open. Molly, was the flap open when you returned?" her father asked.

"Yes. It must have been open all the way because I just ran right inside," she remembered.

"Maybe, when I went back to get my jacket, I forgot to zip the tent as I left," Molly reasoned aloud. "Oh no, it's my own fault," she said and began to sob.

"Don't cry, Sweetheart, we'll keep looking until we find her," Mrs. Brown said as she gathered Molly in her arms.

The rest of the day until dark, other families helped them search the entire campground, even into the shallow part of the pond but nobody found Genie. Some campers continued to help them on Friday, but by Saturday everyone gave up hope. They packed up their camping gear and headed for home.

"Daddy, can we go home a new way? Maybe we will see something interesting to keep me from thinking about Genie?"

So the Brown family exited Hungry Bear Campground through an unfamiliar gate. Not too far from the exit, Mrs. Brown spotted an antique store.

"Look at that nice antique store over there. Let's look around and see if they have anything we might be able to use. We haven't been antiquing for weeks," she said.

"Good Morning travelers, welcome to Mrs. Miller's House of Dolls," the proprietor said.

"Oh my, look at all the dolls. They're everywhere and each one is different from the other," Molly cried out in disbelief.

"Where did you get all these dolls?" she asked.

"Honey, my family has been collecting dolls for over 50 years. Now they are like members of our family. Even our real children help us find them," Mrs. Miller explained.

"Did you ever have a 'Magic Skin Doll by Genius'?" Mrs. Brown asked.

"No. Not until yesterday. You see, late on Friday afternoon, Mr. Miller was working in the fields near the campground when he almost drove the tractor over something in the field. He climbed off the tractor to see what it could be and was shocked to see a beautiful doll laying face down in the dirt. He picked her up and rushed home to show me. We were both so happy she was found before a rain storm made a bigger mess of her," Mrs. Miller explained.

"Wait just a minute and I will show you the precious doll," she said as she hurried to the back of the store.

"I can hardly believe that this doll might be Genie," Molly said, jumping up and down excitedly. Her parents were silently praying that the lost doll was the prize possession.

Molly knew it was Genie even before Mrs. Miller reached them.

"It's her! It's Genie! Look at what the doll is wearing around her neck!" Molly exclaimed as she ran toward Genie and eagerly reached out to take her in her arms to give her doll the biggest hug and kiss she had ever had. The locket around Genie's neck held a beautiful picture of Molly hugging Genie when they first became friends.

Molly took a closer look. "Oh dear, look at the teeth marks in her tummy and look at her legs and arms. They turned dark brown from lying out in the sun," she said crying.

"But, I don't care. I love her more than ever. Now she's really special. Can we please buy her from you, Mrs. Miller?"

"No, you can't buy her from me because she already belongs to you. After all, you are her best friend and you are hers," Mrs. Miller said as she hugged both Molly and Genie and together Molly and Genie hugged and kissed Mrs. Miller in return.

ILLUSTRATION PAGE

ILLUSTRATION PAGE

6

What's A Stranger?

As Sam drove his battery-powered racer down the driveway, a red sports car coasted past his house.

"That man must like the way I drive," Sam thought as he watched the car disappear around the corner for the third time. He raced up the driveway and made a wide turn in front of the open garage.

"Hi, Mr. Sampson," he called when the mail truck pulled up to his mailbox. "Do you have any mail for us today?"

"I sure do," the mailman said as he gathered all the mail for Sam's house. "Look at this big pile."

"Can I put it in the mailbox?" Sam asked.

Mr. Sampson smiled as he handed Sam the pile of letters, magazines, and advertisements. "Do you think you can handle it all?" he asked

"Sure," Sam said as he stuffed the mail into the big black mailbox.

"Good job," the postman said as Sam stepped on the accelerator and waved goodbye.

"Good morning, Sam" Mrs. Blackwell called to him as she took the mail out of her box across the street.

"Hi, Mrs. Blackwell," Sam shouted to her and nearly drove into the street.

She went back into her house just as the red sports car coasted down the street, but this time it pulled up alongside the curb. "Hello, young fellow. How are you today?" the man asked.

Sam smiled. "I'm just fine," he answered as he stopped driving so he could hear what the man was saying.

"That's a mighty nice looking racer you're riding. Come here and show it to me," the man invited.

Sam rode proudly down the driveway to the waiting car.

"Sam, come here! Right now!" his mother hollered from the porch.

He stopped and turned toward her, as the shiny red car sped away from the curb and disappeared out of sight.

His mother ran out of the house and grabbed the front bumper. She tried to pull the racer into the garage, but Sam dragged his feet to keep the racer from moving forward. He cried as he pleaded, "Mommy, Mommy, let go!" When they finally reached the garage, his Mother slammed down the garage door.

She held him close to her and wiped his tears. "I'm sorry, Honey, but I'm afraid I can't let you play outside alone until you learn not to speak to strangers."

"I'm sorry. I promise I won't talk to strangers any more. Please, let me ride my racer," Sam pleaded.

"We'll talk about that later. Right now it's time to buy food and favors for your 5th birthday party tomorrow."

While they shopped, Sam stayed close to his mother. All week he had dreamed about the presents he hoped to get. But now, not riding his electric racer took all the fun out of his birthday.

In the first aisle, his mother picked up some buns and visited with her friend, Sarah Snow. Sam stepped behind his mother and poked at the soft buns.

"Honey, say hello to Mrs. Snow," his Mother said as she pulled him from behind her, but Sam kept still.

"Do you like going shopping with your Mother?" Mrs. Snow asked. Sam hung his head. He didn't answer. He just kept poking the buns.

When they reached the meat counter, his mother chatted with a tall, young man. Sam had never seen him before. Nor had he ever seen anyone with such strange hair.

"Jeremy, this is my son, Sam."

"Hi, Sam. How's it going?" Jeremy asked.

Again, Sam didn't say anything. His mother and Jeremy kept talking so he sat down on the bottom shelf. He wondered why his mother had given him a crabby look. After all, he was keeping his promise.

In the potato chip aisle they met a short, fat man.

"Good morning, Mr. Brinkley. How nice to see you again. You remember my son, don't you?"

"Why of course. We met at your house when I came over to fix your lawnmower. Young man, you certainly have grown. Are you having fun this summer?"

Sam didn't answer even though his mother kept saying, "Answer Mr. Brinkley's question!" Instead he crossed his arms and closed his mouth real tight and pouted.

"I wish everyone would stop asking me questions," he said to himself. "Since I don't know what a stranger is, I'm not going to talk to anyone so I can drive my car! I have to keep the promise I made to my mother," he told himself.

When they reached the check-out counter, the grocery cart was filled with chocolate cake mix, birthday candles, clown napkins, vanilla ice cream, Kool Aid, nuts, hot dogs, buns, potato chips, and party favors.

"It looks to me like someone is going to have a birthday party," the young clerk said. "How old are you going to be?"

Sam crouched behind the cart and kept quiet. He was certain that this girl was a stranger. She looked a lot different than anyone he had ever seen before. She even talked funny. His mother whispered something to him, but Sam couldn't hear what she said. A baby in the cart behind him was screaming.

When they reached the car, his mother loaded the groceries into the trunk. Sam climbed into the car. When his bare legs touched the leather seat he jumped up and bumped his head. The blazing summer sun had made the seats too hot to sit on.

"Sam, what's the matter with you?" his mother asked him when she got into the car.

"The seat is too hot," he answered.

"No, I mean, why didn't you speak to those nice people when they spoke to you? You're usually so friendly."

Sam sat on the edge of the seat. He picked at the scab on his knee. "I was just keeping my promise," he said quietly.

"What promise?" she asked

"The promise not to speak to strangers," he said proudly.

"Honey, those people aren't strangers. They're my friends."

"They're not strangers?" he asked frowning.

"No, Sam, people are not strangers when I'm with you and when I speak to them."

Sam cocked his head and bit on his lower lip.

"You mean, when I'm with you I can talk to people you know, even if I don't know them?" He stopped picking on his scab and looked up at his mother.

"Why of course," she assured him.

"Were you mad at me for helping Mr. Sampson with the mail?"

"Of course not, Honey."

He still didn't understand what a stranger was.

"Were you mad at me for talking to Mrs. Blackwell?"

"No, I wasn't angry at you for talking to our neighbor."

Finally, he asked, "Was the man in the shiny, red car the only stranger I shouldn't have talked to today?"

His mother pulled him close to her. She gave him a big hug.

"That's right, Sam. I'm sorry. I thought you understood what the word 'stranger' meant. Besides, I wasn't angry with you. I was only frightened when I saw you talking to someone we don't know. Now, let's fasten our seat belts. It's time to get home."

"Can I play outside by myself and ride my racer?" he asked.

"Yes, Sam, and while you ride your racer, I'll bake a chocolate birthday cake for a little boy who grew up in a big way today."

Sam bounced up and down cheering, "Hurray! Hurray! Yippee!"

He fastened his seat belt and sat up straight. When his mother squeezed his hand, Sam smiled the most grown-up smile he had ever smiled.

ILLUSTRATION PAGE

ILLUSTRATION PAGE

7

Contact With Joey

"Those dumb clothes I'm supposed to wear on Sunday are probably in the hamper. Hey look! Here are my favorite red sweatpants. They'll do just as well. I'll put them on backwards, so the dirty knees won't show. Darn! Now I can't find my other shoe," Joey mumbled to himself.

"Joey, hurry up! It's time to leave for church," his Mother called to him from the bottom of the stairs.

"Oh, nuts! Why do I have to go to church? We never do anything interesting. It's all just a big bore," he griped.

"Joey, hurry up. We're all in the car waiting for you," she called again.

"I wish she'd stop yelling at me. Everyone's always harping at me. Now, where's my leather army jacket? Oh, here it is under the bed."

"Joey!"

"I'm coming. I'm coming. Hold your horses," Joey shouted back.

"I'll just wear my tennis shoes. Comfort, that's what I like, comfort. Shucks, the lace is missing. Oh, well, I'll just curl up my toes. That'll keep them on my feet," he told himself as he stumbled down the stairs and hobbled over to the car.

"Well, it's about time. Joey, why in the world are you wearing those terrible clothes?" his Dad asked.

"It's all I could find on short notice," Joey explained.

As he squeezed into the family car he complained, "I wish we'd get a bigger car."

"Joey, quit pushing your brothers."

"I'm not pushing. I'm just trying to get in far enough to close the door."

"Why does everyone always pick on me?" Joey grumbled to himself. "I can't wait to get out of this car."

Finally, they reached the church, found a parking space and went inside.

"Oh, there's that pushy friend of Mom's. What's she doing here?"

"Good morning, Joey," she said as she looked him over in a critical way.

"I wish she wouldn't talk to me. I don't feel like talking."

"Hey, there's Mike. What a nerd! Look at those spiffy clothes. Bet he'd rather have on sweats. I'll just go over and talk to good old Mike since everyone else is ignoring me. I hate this place. They're a bunch of phonies. All prim and proper, but they can't even look or smile at me."

"Hi, Mike."

"Hi, Joey," Mike mumbled as he looked away.

"He doesn't seem too friendly. I'll give him a poke. That'll get his attention. Whoops! Here comes the music teacher. I sure hate to sing. It's so boring. I've got to get out of here quickly," he decided.

"Children, let's move closer to the piano," the music teacher instructed.

"Good, here's my chance," he tried to scoot out before she caught him.

"Joey, where are you going?" the teacher asked.

"Got to go to the bathroom," Joey said over his shoulder as he left the room.

"The great escape! I'll come back when the singing's over."

"Good. Here's a nice clean wall to doodle on while I'm in here," Joey said as he hid in the toilet stall. When the music stopped, he hurried back into the room and slipped in between Mike and Paul. "They won't mind. They like me," he told himself.

"Hey, Joey, what do you think you're doing?" the boys asked indignantly.

"It's a free country. I can sit wherever I want."

"Well, not between us. You smell!"

"Joey, please quiet down and stop bothering Mike and Paul," the teacher said.

"Boring! Boring! Now what boring video do we have to watch?" he complained.

"Joey, is that you pushing?" the teacher asked when the lights were turned off.

"Boy, that lady must have cat eyes. She sees in the dark."

The screen showed the title of the lesson BAKING BREAD.

"What's such a big deal about baking bread? You just go to the store and buy some. Big deal!" he muttered to himself.

Just then a huge field of grain showed on the screen. "Wow! That field must be a thousand acres and look at all those monster machines riding back and forth cutting the waving, yellow grain. That's quite a sight!" Joey was hooked.

When the harvesting was finished, Joey was really captivated by the next part as the film explained how the grain became flour and how the flour turned into bread. "Cool! I never dreamed so much went into baking bread. Not so boring after all, I have to admit," he said to his friends when the lights were turned on.

"Joey, how did class go today?" his mother asked as the family stuffed themselves back into the car.

"It was okay, I guess. We learned a bunch of stuff about bread. Can we make some when we get home?"

"No, but how about baking some bread after supper tonight?" she suggested.

Everyone cheered!

"By the way, was the teacher upset about your clothes?"

"No, she didn't say anything, but I guess I'll wear my Sunday clothes next week, if I can find them."

ILLUSTRATION PAGE

ILLUSTRATION PAGE

8

The King's Kids

Once upon a time, in the land of joy and sorrow, there reigned a King who had twin sons. Cornelius was handsome to behold, intelligent, strong and eager for life. Everyone pampered him and praised him.

One the other hand, Aloysius was born handicapped and left to fend for himself. Each day while Cornelius charmed the court with his good looks, intelligent answers and charming ways; Aloysius hid behind the royal throne and listened to the affairs of state.

On the day the boys turned six, two mysterious boxes arrived at the palace. As the court gathered, the trumpets sounded and the jester tumbled.

"Hear Ye! Hear Ye!" the King proclaimed. "Today, I honor each of my sons with a beautiful box to celebrate their birthdays. The gold box I present to Cornelius and the silver box I present to Aloysius. Each day they shall be allowed to open one of the envelopes which lay inside each box."

"Let the drums roll! Let the celebration begin!" he shouted and the drums rolled.

Cornelius looked at the box and then he looked at Aloysius. Aloysius looked at his box and then he looked at Cornelius. They shrugged their shoulders and waited. Then the trumpets blared.

The King held his scepter high in the air while everyone waited quietly. When he lowered it, the boys knew it was time to open their boxes. Slowly the King lowered his scepter and slowly Cornelius and

Aloysius raised the lids of their beautiful gold and silver boxes and peeked inside.

There lay an exquisitely hand engraved envelope with the word "GOLD" written on it. A note was attached to each envelope which read: "Take this coin and do with it what you wish."

Cornelius took out the gold piece, caressed it with his finger, threw the envelope on the floor, thrust the coin it into his pocket, and ran from the room.

On the second day, as the king entered the throne room the trumpets blared and the court gathered. Drums rolled to announce the arrival of Cornelius and Aloysius who picked up their boxes when they reached the foot of the throne.

"Today my sons will open their second envelope. Let the trumpets sound," the King proclaimed as he raised his scepter high in the air. When he lowered his scepter, the boys opened their boxes.

The word "FRANKINCENSE" was engraved on the second envelope. Inside the envelope each one found a fragrant smelling gum resin. The note read: "Take it and do with it what you wish."

Cornelius removed the resin and jammed it into his pants pocket. Then he crumbled the envelope and sulked out of the room.

Aloysius fingered the unusual object, carefully returned it to the envelope, thanked his Father, and left the room deep in thought.

On the third day, the trumpets called the court into session as the King entered the throne room. The drums rolled to announce the arrival of Cornelius and Aloysius. When they reached the throne they picked up their boxes as the King proclaimed. "Today my sons will open their boxes for the third and last time. Let the trumpets sound," he shouted as he raised his scepter.

When he lowered his scepter, the boys opened their gold and silver boxes for the third and last time. Inside, lay the third envelope engraved with the word "MYRRH." The note read: "Take it and do with it what you wish."

Cornelius tore open the envelope, saw the Myrrh, threw the envelope and the box on floor, and ran crying from the room. Aloysius opened the envelope, studied the fragrant bitter sweet resin which lay inside, thanked his Father, and continued to sniff the resin as he wandered out of the room.

THIS IS WHAT EACH GIFT MEANS:

A *gold coin* is a symbol which stands for great wealth.

Frankincense is a sweet smelling gum resin used as incense during religious ceremonies.

Myrrh is an expensive spice used in making perfume, medicine, incense and to anoint the dead.

Now think about the questions below and create an ending to the story.

WHEN THE SON'S RECEIVED THEIR GIFTS, WHICH SON'S ATTITUDE DO YOU THINK WAS MOST PLEASING TO THE FATHER?
      a.) Cornelius   b.) Aloysius

WHICH SON DO YOU THINK WAS THE WISEST?
      a.) Cornelius   b.) Aloysius

WHICH SON DID YOU LIKE THE MOST AND WHY?
      a.) Cornelius   b.) Aloysius

WHICH SON BECAME THE NEXT KING?
      a.) Cornelius   b.) Aloysius

WHY WOULD YOU CHOOSE HIM TO BE KING?

Write your own reasons here:

On the following pages draw your pictures of the story.

ILLUSTRATION PAGE

ILLUSTRATION PAGE